for my pal Linda! ♡ ♡

THE
Adventures
OF
Grandma
Charlotte!

Life is an adventure!

♡ Marla S.

D1473244

©2018 by Marla Stahl
All rights reserved.
www.woofbooks.com

THE Adventures OF Grandma Charlotte!

By Marla Stahl

Illustrated by Haylea Weiss

Once there were two very nice grandmas who were friends.
One was Grandma Shirley and the other was Grandma Charlotte.
They were best friends. They met each other at an exercise class
in New Jersey. Yep, New Jersey!

That's where they lived.

They got along famously, which really means... they were very silly together in class! The two grandmas liked to make up silly words to the music and do silly dances when they exercised. They were so funny! They made everyone around them laugh!

Grandma Shirley wanted to invite Grandma Charlotte to lunch one day, but she realized she didn't have Grandma Charlotte's phone number. But she remembered seeing Grandma Charlotte's unusual license plates on her car—KHAATZ—and thought that must be Grandma Charlotte's last name.

"Yeah, that's it—Mrs. Charlotte Khaatz!"

But for some reason, that listing could not be found. "Well," she thought, "maybe the number is private!"

So at the next exercise class, she mentioned this to Grandma Charlotte, who roared with laughter and explained that she was one of those "cat ladies." Yep! Grandma Charlotte LOVED cats, and she had many of them! And she decided to tell the world about her love for cats on her license plates—but she spelled it a funny way: KHAATZ, instead of CATS. (Obviously, Grandma Charlotte loved being silly, even if she wasn't in class!) It wasn't her last name after all!

The grandmas exchanged phone numbers, and after that day they went out for coffee, lunch, shopping, and silliness all the time. And they were still very silly in their exercise class, too, making everyone laugh with their silly songs and dances, and even making silly faces!

Grandma Charlotte used to be a teacher. She loved teaching the 4th grade, where she learned a lot from her students about making silly faces! She finally decided to retire after teaching for 40 years. Yep, 40 years! Then she enjoyed planting flowers in her garden, and teaching people how to take care of their own gardens. But after a while, she missed doing super-meaningful things that helped others, so she decided to volunteer all around the world, helping people and studying animals. Even though cats were her favorite, she loved all animals!

Grandma Charlotte enjoyed sharing her stories with Grandma Shirley about her many adventures. Grandma Shirley loved hearing about these adventures, but they were things that she would never, ever do—like:

...riding on sea turtles in the Galapagos Islands...

...sleeping on the jungle floor with large spiders hanging above her...

...floating down rivers on rafts in exotic places, and getting bitten not once, but twice on the same trip by a magical jumping fish which, legend has it, only jumps up and bites people once every 100 years!...

...flying in a hot air balloon over the Serengeti in Africa and blowing kisses to all the wild animals (she especially loved the lions!)...

...and studying animals like bugs and lemurs and black bears in the forest. That's just to name a few!

And every time Grandma Shirley heard the details, especially things like dangling spiders and jumping fish, she said something like:

"That is REASON #972 why I don't take these trips with you!"

Apparently Grandma Shirley was not quite as adventurous a grandma as Grandma Charlotte was! And she REALLY didn't like spiders!

The only trip she would have enjoyed was when Grandma Charlotte went to an orphanage in Romania and got to hug babies all day. Grandma Shirley would have LOVED that! After all, she was one of the best grandmas in town! But her idea of a real adventure was watching The Weather Channel. Who can blame her? Those storms are something else!

When Grandma Charlotte and Grandma Shirley decided to move to new homes to live closer to their families, each one was sad to say goodbye. But guess what? Every week the two of them talked on the telephone for at least an hour! They were still good friends, and could still be silly and laugh together.

Grandma Charlotte still shared stories about her adventures, and the two grandmas laughed and laughed!

One day Grandma Charlotte told Grandma Shirley a big secret. Do you want to know what it is?

Are you sure?

Here is the big secret:

As much as she loved all of her many fun adventures, Grandma Charlotte's very favorite thing to do was to be at home near her family... sitting in her favorite chair... snuggling with her cats... drinking tea... and laughing with her dear friend, Grandma Shirley, on the telephone!

Now, that's the kind of adventure any grandma could love!

What can we learn from Grandma Charlotte and Grandma Shirley?

1. The two grandmas show us that we can have fun adventures no matter how old we are or what we like to do. Sometimes, just learning something new is a fun adventure. Grandma Shirley learned a lot about weather on The Weather Channel. She also liked doing challenging puzzles and learning new languages. She especially had fun learning how to speak Italian! Using your brain is always an adventure. Grandma Shirley was really good at that!

Do you speak another language? Which one(s)?

_____

What is your favorite kind of adventure? You can write it here:

_____

_____

_____

2. Grandma Charlotte went to many new places. See if you can find the Galapagos Islands and the Serengeti on a map, and write down the kinds of animals you might find there.

In the Galapagos Islands, you might find these animals:

_____

_____

_____

In the Serengeti, you might find these animals:

_____

_____

_____